# WE'RE OFF TO FIND THE WITCH'S HOUSE

**Mr. Krieb**

illustrated by **R.W. Alley**

PUFFIN BOOKS

PUFFIN BOOKS
Published by the Penguin Group
Penguin Young Readers Group, 345 Hudson Street, New York, New York 10014, U.S.A.
Penguin Group (Canada), 90 Eglinton Avenue East, Suite 700, Toronto, Ontario, Canada M4P 2Y3
(a division of Pearson Penguin Canada Inc.)
Penguin Books Ltd, 80 Strand, London WC2R 0RL, England
Penguin Ireland, 25 St Stephen's Green, Dublin 2, Ireland
(a division of Penguin Books Ltd)
Penguin Group (Australia), 250 Camberwell Road, Camberwell, Victoria 3124, Australia
(a division of Pearson Australia Group Pty Ltd)
Penguin Books India Pvt Ltd, 11 Community Centre, Panchsheel Park, New Delhi - 110 017, India
Penguin Group (NZ), Cnr Airborne and Rosedale Roads, Albany, Auckland 1310, New Zealand
(a division of Pearson New Zealand Ltd)
Penguin Books (South Africa) (Pty) Ltd, 24 Sturdee Avenue, Rosebank, Johannesburg 2196, South Africa

Registered Offices: Penguin Books Ltd, 80 Strand, London WC2R 0RL, England

First published in the United States of America by Dutton Children's Books, a division of Penguin Young Readers Group, 2005
Published by Puffin Books, a division of Penguin Young Readers Group, 2007

3  5  7  9  10  8  6  4  2

CIP Data is available.

Puffin Books ISBN 978-0-14-240854-4

Designed by Tim Hall     Manufactured in China

To all the delightful children with whom, for thirty years, I shared the tricks of imagination and the treats of language and laughter. Many now have children of their own who will soon be off to find the witch's house!

Mr. Krieb

For the tricksters and treaters of Hampden Meadows

R.W.A.

We're off to find the witch's house.

**Which house?**

**The witch's house.**

We're off to find the witch's house,
but we're not afraid.

No, we're not afraid.

We're creeping down the witch's street.

Which street? The witch's street.

We're creeping down the witch's street,
but we're not afraid.
No, we're not afraid.

We're slinking by a blinking owl, a winking owl, a blinking owl.

Wave good-bye to the winking owl, watching with one eye.

We're skedaddling past a skeleton,
a skittle-skattling skeleton,
a skinny, grinning skeleton, shake-rattling its bones.

We're bolting by big Frankenstein,
the herky-jerky, lurching kind—

his heavy head held on with twine.
Watch out! Don't get too close!

We're galloping past a ghastly ghost,
a mostly misty, ghostly ghost,

a flying, floating, twisty ghost,
swishing through the dark.

We're rambling past a howling wolf,
a scowling wolf, a growling wolf,

a hairy, scary, glaring wolf,
prowling in the park.

We're scrambling past Count Dracula,
a shirking, lurking Dracula,

with flowing cape spectacular
and fangs that glow so bright.

'Cause we're coming to the witch's house.
Which house?
The witch's house.
We're coming to the witch's house,
with bats and spiderwebs.

We're knocking on the witch's door.
Which door?
The witch's door.

We're knocking on the witch's door.

It opens with a . . .

# SCREECH!

There she is—she's standing there!
She's standing where?
She's standing there!
There she is—she's standing there!

And we all scream . . .

Trick